To Arden, Arlene, Alisan, Allison, Caroline, Nancy & Susan—
It takes a long time to grow a friend.
—R.S.

For Cristina, we were *mint* to be best friends.
—H.H.

Dial Books for Young Readers
An imprint of Penguin Random House LLC, New York

First published in the United States of America by Dial Books for Young Readers,
an imprint of Penguin Random House LLC, 2021

Text copyright © 2021 by Ruth Spiro
Illustrations copyright © 2021 by Holly Hatam

Visit us online at penguinrandomhouse.com.

Library of Congress Cataloging-in-Publication Data is available.

Manufactured in China
ISBN 9780399186301

1 3 5 7 9 10 8 6 4 2

Design by Mina Chung • Text set in Napoleone Slab ITC

Maxine and the Greatest Garden Ever!

written by
Ruth Spiro

illustrated by
Holly Hatam

Ever!

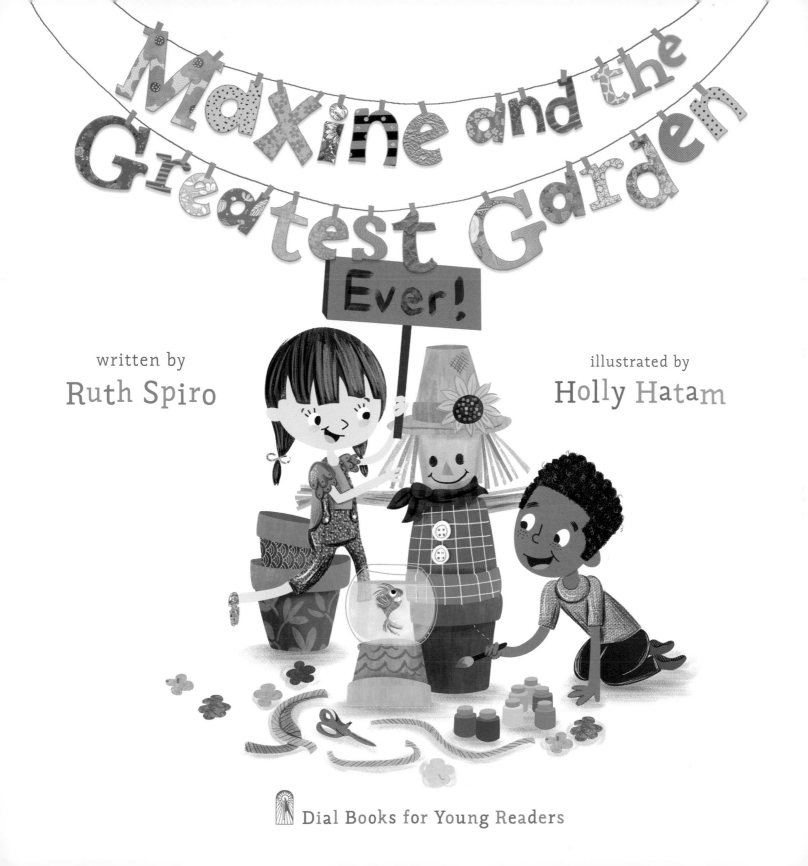

Dial Books for Young Readers

Maxine and Milton made
a perfect pair.

I WAS READING A
BOOK ON HELIUM. I
COULDN'T PUT IT DOWN.

Molecool!
H_2O

Certificate
1
Best Behaved
Pet

When Maxine was bored,
Milton made her laugh.

When Milton was hungry,
Maxine served up snacks with style.

And whenever they heard their favorite song . . .

Maxine liked making things, and she especially liked making things for Milton.

"If I can dream it, I can build it!" she said.

Lucky for her, Milton provided plenty of inspiration.

Sometimes their friend Leo came over.
Leo liked making things too.
Just . . . in a different way.

One day, they made an exciting discovery.
"Let's make a garden," said Leo.
"Let's make The Greatest Garden Ever!"
Milton grinned from gill to gill. He hoped the new garden would also include a pond.

First, they drew their designs.
Leo's was pretty.

Maxine's was practical.

Next, they planted.
Maxine thought Leo's seeds looked lonely.
Leo thought Maxine's seemed squished.

Lucky for Milton, the one thing they agreed on was his pond.

Every day
they watered

and waited.

And waited. Until they had grown . . .

The Greatest Garden Ever!

But their garden had other admirers . . .

"What happened?" cried Leo.

"Animals!" said Maxine. "Let's make something to keep them away!"

"Something that looks nice?" asked Leo.

"Something that works."

They sculpted and stuffed,

fitted and fluffed.

"Can you make it move?" asked Leo. Maxine thought that was a silly question.

Unfortunately, the animals didn't know
they were supposed to be afraid.

"You were supposed to keep them away," said Leo to the scarecrow. "You didn't help."

"Maybe he did," said Maxine. "Now we know what doesn't work. That's important too."

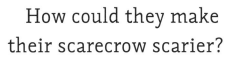

How could they make
their scarecrow scarier?

They hammered and hitched, measured and switched.

Then while Leo sewed,
Maxine wrote some code.

They made a

critter-creeping,

laser-tripping,

disco-ball-blinking,

tuba-tooting...

This time it worked . . . a little too well.

"Your circuits made the tuba too tooty!" said Leo.
"Your disco ball made the lights too blinky!" said Maxine.

IT'S ALL YOUR FAULT!

And that was the end of that.

The next day, Maxine couldn't stop thinking about the garden.
All that hard work . . . and now everything was a big mess.

She had to make things better,
and she wanted to start with Leo.
Because it takes a long time to grow a garden . . .

but even longer to grow a friend.

"You're right," she said. "The tuba was too tooty."
"I messed up too," Leo replied. "My bright idea was . . .
too bright."

They nibbled on the last of the lettuce and thought about how to fix the garden.

Meanwhile, Milton made his "Feed Me" face.

"Hungry? We can share!"

"The animals . . . that's why they keep coming back," said Maxine. "Milton, you're the smartest fish ever!"

With a better design, they wouldn't need a scarecrow. "If I make this work, can you make it look nice?" Leo thought that was a silly question.

First, they un-stuffed the scarecrow.

Then they repaired,

replanted,
and redecorated.

Finally, Leo adjusted the audio.
"Finished!"

"Almost," said Maxine.
"We need one more thing . . ."

Best
Buds

Achieve
Grapeness